GOOD·BYE
hello

Hello and many happy days
to Laura and Brack together
—B.S.H.

For Alex
—M.B.

Harcourt

Orlando   Boston   Dallas   Chicago   San Diego

Visit *The Learning Site!*
www.harcourtschool.com

GOOD-BYE
hello

by BARBARA SHOOK HAZEN
illustrated by MICHAEL BRYANT

We're moving, so I
have to say good-bye.
Good-bye for good, old neighborhood.

Good-bye, swings. Good-bye, park.
Good-bye, corner Mini-Mart.

Good-bye, sidewalk. Good-bye, street.
Good-bye, McBurger's for a treat.

Good-bye, pigeon. Good-bye, tree.
Good-bye, cat that follows me.

Good-bye, doorman at the door.
I won't come through here anymore.

Good-bye, secret hiding spot.
I'll miss you an awful lot.

Good-bye, my room most of all,
with all my drawings on the wall.
Good-bye, bed that got too small.

Good-bye, toy shelves.
Good-bye, rocks.
Good-bye, baby books and blocks,

But not to you, Fuzzy Bear.
How did you end up in there?

Good-bye, neighbors that I know,
the Shooks above, the Changs below,
and Mrs. McGrady, the cookie lady.

Good-bye, Jamie.
That's when I start to cry
and hate good-bye.

I'm sad awhile after we go,
until it's time to say hello.

Hello, brand-new neighborhood
with a Pizza Pit and a Toys Are Good.

Hello, new park with a pond
and a great big hill for sledding on.

Hello, yard. Hello, tree.

You're just the perfect size for me.

Hello, squirrel. Don't run away.

Maybe we'll be friends someday.

Hello, mailbox with our name.

Hello, rooms that *aren't* the same.

Hello, walls. Hello, staircase.
Hello, new secret hiding place.

Hello, my new room upstairs.
Hello, new bed; hello, old chairs.

Hello, window. Hello, view—
There's a bird's nest and some people, too.

Hello, new neighbors at the door.
Hello, I'm Terry. Let's explore.

Hello, attic. Hello, drum.
Hello, tent and aquarium.

Hello, boxes with all sorts
of things so we can make a fort.

Hello, Jamie, guess what!
I miss you. But I like it here a lot,
and I can't wait for you to come.

The three of us will really have fun.

This edition is published by special arrangement with Atheneum Books for Young Readers, Simon & Schuster Children's Publishing Division.

Grateful acknowledgment is made to Atheneum Books for Young Readers, Simon & Schuster Children's Publishing Division for permission to reprint *Good-Bye Hello* by Barbara Shook Hazen, illustrated by Michael Bryant. Text copyright © 1995 by Barbara Shook Hazen; illustrations copyright © 1995 by Michael Bryant.

Printed in the United States of America

ISBN 0-15-313411-9

9 10 179 02